BRAVO, MAURICE!

Rebecca Bond

Megan Tingley Books

 Little, Brown and Company
Boston New York London

For my favorite father,
Duncan

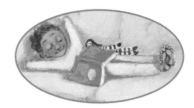

First Edition

Library of Congress Cataloging-in-Publication Data
Bond, Rebecca.
 Bravo, Maurice! / Rebecca Bond. — 1st ed.
  p. cm.
 Summary: Since he was a baby, all the members of Maurice's family think he
will take up their careers, until one day they discover he has a special gift of his
own.
 ISBN 0-316-10545-7
 [1. Occupations—Fiction. 2. Family life—Fiction. 3. Sound—Fiction. 4. City and
town life—Fiction.] I. Title.
PZ7.B63686Br 2000
[E] — dc21   99-29855

10 9 8 7 6 5 4 3 2 1

Printed in Singapore

The illustrations for this book were done in acrylic.
The text was set in Legacy Serif, and the display type was handlettered.

One August evening, in a small, high apartment, in the hot, bustling city, something wonderful happened. Mama and Papa Marcela brought their baby boy home. His name was Maurice Duncan Marcela, and he had just been born.

When Mama and Papa and Maurice arrived at their apartment, it was crowded with aunts, uncles, grandparents, cousins, and friends who had come especially to be there when Maurice came home for the first time.

Everyone squeezed in to look. *What is he going to be like?* they all wondered.

"Look! He has my large hands!" exclaimed Papa. "He'll be a baker, just like me."

"He has my watchful eyes!" whispered Mama. "He'll be a writer, just like me."

"But look at his toes!" laughed Uncle Eddie. "They tap and twiddle like mine. He'll be a taxi driver, just like me!"

"Don't miss that nose! It's delicate like mine," smiled Grandmother Marcela. "He'll be a gardener, just like me."

Maurice fit comfortably into the Marcela household, full of talking and laughing, cooking and clinking plates.

Even after Maurice had gone to bed, he loved to listen to the comforting sounds all around him. He listened to Uncle Eddie whistling and the soft whirring of Grandmother Marcela's sewing machine. He listened to trucks rumbling and dogs barking outside on the streets below. And every once in a while Maurice heard a marvelous thing that made him wrap his arms around himself and listen very closely. It was the sound of singing voices. They drifted up to him through his open window, like the sweet smell of bread rising from a bakery.

As he listened, sometimes Maurice would sing along.

As Maurice grew older, everyone in his family was eager to take him into the worlds they knew outside the apartment. They wanted to show Maurice all the things they loved to do.

First, Uncle Eddie took Maurice out in his taxi into the hum of downtown.

"With your tapping toes, Maurice, like mine," Uncle Eddie chuckled, "you were meant to be a taxi driver. Just you wait."

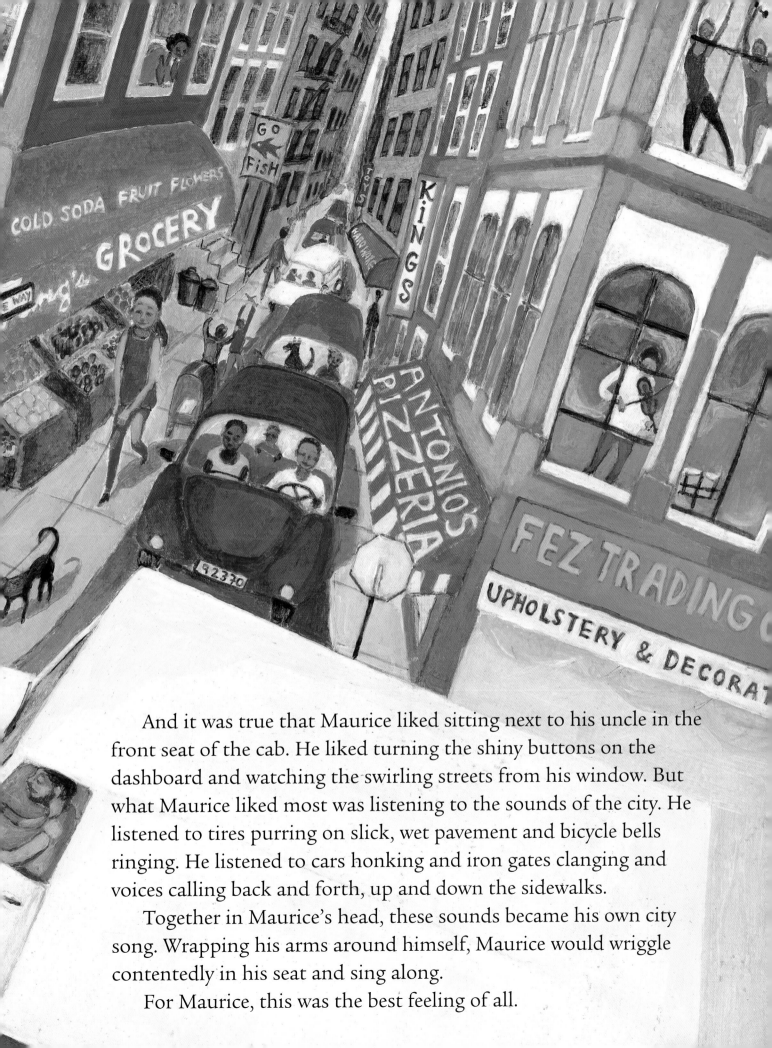

And it was true that Maurice liked sitting next to his uncle in the front seat of the cab. He liked turning the shiny buttons on the dashboard and watching the swirling streets from his window. But what Maurice liked most was listening to the sounds of the city. He listened to tires purring on slick, wet pavement and bicycle bells ringing. He listened to cars honking and iron gates clanging and voices calling back and forth, up and down the sidewalks.

Together in Maurice's head, these sounds became his own city song. Wrapping his arms around himself, Maurice would wriggle contentedly in his seat and sing along.

For Maurice, this was the best feeling of all.

Soon, Papa introduced Maurice to his bakery. It was early in the morning, and the bakery already smelled good.

"What do you say we try out those large baker hands of yours?" Papa asked, winking. "I know you will like it here."

And it was true that Maurice liked working alongside all the other bakers. He liked rolling out the powdery hunks of dough and cutting the thick biscuits.

But what Maurice liked most was listening to the sounds of the bakery. He listened to the soft, floury pat of dough being flipped and kneaded, the rasping ring of a whisk circling the sides of a metal bowl, the damp crunch of nuts being ground to meal. Together, in Maurice's head, these sounds became the music of the morning bakery. Quietly, as he kneaded great mounds of dough, Maurice would sing along.

For Maurice, this was the best feeling of all.

One day, Mama and Maurice took the subway together to her office. "A writer needs to watch the world carefully," Mama whispered to Maurice. "Noticing everything, like a spy. With your watchful eyes like mine, you will be good at this."

And it was true that Maurice noticed many things in the busy office. He noticed the walls covered with notes, and the half-eaten lunches, and the way the light changed in the window at the end of the day.

But no matter where he went, what Maurice noticed most were the
sounds in the old building. From every room there erupted the noises of
furiously tapping typing and constantly ringing phones. Fast footsteps
went clickity-clicking down the halls. And chairs squeaked and groaned
as writers leaned back to think. Together, in Maurice's head, these
sounds became the office orchestra.

   Lulled by the babble of machines and the buzz of movement,
Maurice would sing along.

   For Maurice, this was the best feeling of all.

"It takes a good nose to know a good flower," Grandmother Marcela told Maurice. "And with your delicate nose like mine, you have just the right equipment. You will make a fine gardener, I'm sure."

That weekend, Grandmother Marcela led Maurice into the greenhouse where she worked, behind the Morning Glory Garden Shop.

And it was true that Maurice loved drifting from flower to flower like a honeybee and smelling the sugary scents.

But what Maurice liked most was listening to the sounds of the warm, moist greenhouse. He listened to the crisp clipping of pruning shears and the chirping and caroling of visiting sparrows. He listened to the sprinkler hissing a steady stream of mist. And he listened to the summer rain, drumming down like thousands of tiny feet on the thick greenhouse glass.

Together the sounds of the greenhouse danced in Maurice's head. As he settled in among the papery petals and deep-green leaves, Maurice sang contentedly along.

For Maurice, this was the best feeling of all.

And so it was that Maurice spent his days in Uncle Eddie's taxi and Papa's bakery, in Mama's office and Grandmother Marcela's greenhouse. Everyone was pleased that Maurice fit so smoothly into their worlds. And in secret, they each believed they knew what this meant. *When he grew up, Maurice was going to be just like them.*

Then one August evening, in a small, high apartment, in the hot, bustling city, something wonderful happened. As the sky outside turned a pearly silver pink, Mama and Papa, Uncle Eddie, and Grandmother Marcela gathered in the kitchen, cooking together and talking, as they did on many nights.

Down the hall, Maurice settled into a bath. It was very quiet.
But in the stillness, Maurice felt as though something was missing.
He began to think about the clattering city songs of Uncle Eddie's
taxi. He thought about the soft, floury patting sounds of Papa's
morning bakery. He thought about the thrilling buzz of Mama's
busy office, and the quick chirping and clipping of Grandmother's
lush greenhouse.

And all at once, Maurice began to sing along to the chorus in his head. His clear, smooth voice rose in a great swell, filling the air in the small bathroom. It pushed against the walls and floor and ceiling, and overflowed out into the evening air.

Mama heard it first.

"Listen," she whispered, touching Papa on the arm.

Together they stood still and listened to the wondrous sounds rolling down the hall and into their steamy kitchen. It was like nothing they had ever heard before.

Looking around at one another, all at once they knew. Maurice did have Uncle Eddie's tapping toes and Papa's large hands. He did have Mama's watchful eyes and Grandmother Marcela's delicate nose. But Maurice had something all his own, too. He had a voice as sweet and as clear and as rich as a fine golden honey.

When Maurice stepped out of the bathroom, he was met with the clap-
ping and cheering of his proud family. They hugged Maurice and kissed
him and laughed. They lifted him high into the air and twirled him around
like a king.